DREAMWORKS

DRAGONS

Gift of the
NIGHT
FURY

adapted by Maggie Testa

SIMON SPOTLIGHT

New York London Toronto Sydney New Delhi

SIMON SPOTLIGHT
An imprint of Simon & Schuster Children's Publishing Division
1230 Avenue of the Americas, New York, New York 10020
How to Train Your Dragon © 2014 DreamWorks Animation L.L.C.
All rights reserved, including the right of reproduction in whole or in part in any form.
SIMON SPOTLIGHT and colophon are registered trademarks of Simon & Schuster, Inc.
For information about special discounts for bulk purchases, please contact Simon & Schuster Special Sales
at 1-866-506-1949 or business@simonandschuster.com.
Manufactured in the United States of America 0714 LAK
1 2 3 4 5 6 7 8 9 10 First Edition
ISBN 978-1-4814-0436-5
ISBN 978-1-4814-0437-2 (eBook)

Everyone in Berk was in a jolly mood. The annual winter holiday, Snoggletog, was fast approaching. Decorations and lights were going up all over the village and this year's celebration was sure to be one to remember now that Vikings and dragons were living in harmony.

Early one morning, a few days before Snoggletog, Hiccup and Toothless went flying, just like they always did. Hiccup helped Toothless fly by controlling the mechanical tail he had made for his dragon.

The best friends were practicing some new tricks when all of a sudden hundreds of Berk's dragons flew past them, all going in the opposite direction. One of the dragons got so close, it knocked Hiccup's helmet right off his head. Toothless dove down after the helmet, but Hiccup knew there was no time.

"We'll get it later, bud," he told Toothless. "Right now we need to get back and find out what's going on."

Back in Berk, the Vikings were panicking.

"What's going on?" cried Astrid, one of Hiccup's best friends.

"Why are the dragons flying away?" someone else asked. "What if they never come back?"

"Where are all of our dragons going?" asked Stoick, the chief of Berk and Hiccup's father.

The Vikings gathered in the Great Hall.
"Snoggletog is ruined!" someone yelled.
But Stoick knew better. "We've been perfectly
happy celebrating Snoggletog without dragons for
generations, and there's no reason we can't do it again.
We don't know where our dragons have gone off to,
but we have to have faith that they'll be back soon."

The Vikings weren't so sure, but what choice did
they have? Snoggletog would have to go on without
the dragons.

That night, Hiccup and his friends walked sadly through the village. It seemed so empty without the dragons. The only one of Hiccup's friends who didn't seem sad was Fishlegs. No one knew what that was about, and Fishlegs wasn't telling.

"I have an idea," Astrid spoke up. "Let's come up with a bunch of new holiday traditions to bury the sadness."

"You might be on to something," Hiccup agreed with her.

"Easy for you to say," Tuffnut said to Hiccup. "Your dragon can't go anywhere without you."

Hiccup knew Tuffnut was right. It wasn't fair that Toothless couldn't fly without him. So he made a new tail for his dragon—one that Toothless could use to fly on his own.

The next morning Hiccup gave the new tail to Toothless. It didn't take long for Toothless to get used to it. Then—*whoosh*—Toothless flew off into the sky . . . without Hiccup.

Three days later, Toothless still hadn't returned to Berk. Hiccup felt sadder than he had in a long time.

He was wandering around the village when he saw Fishlegs carrying a large basket of fish into a barn.

What's that about? Hiccup wondered.

Soon Fishlegs exited the barn. His basket of fish was gone. Once the coast was clear, Hiccup peeked through the barn doors, curious to see what was inside.

And that's when Fishlegs's Gronckle dragon, Meatlug, burst out of the barn and flew high up into the air, taking Hiccup along for the ride.

"Hiccup, where are you going?" Astrid yelled to her friend.

"But what about presents, Meatlug?" Fishlegs called to his escaping dragon.

But Meatlug and Hiccup were already too far away to hear them. Astrid, Fishlegs, and the rest of Hiccup's friends wandered into the barn, where they found a pile of eggs—Meatlug's eggs.

That gave Astrid an idea for a new Snoggletog tradition. Since everyone in Berk was missing their dragons, they could give everyone a dragon egg as a present!

Meanwhile, Meatlug and Hiccup arrived at a nearby island. All of Berk's dragons were there—except Toothless—and there were lots and lots of baby dragons. Everywhere Hiccup looked a new dragon was hatching. Now Hiccup understood why all the dragons had left Berk—this island was where they came to have babies.

Hiccup watched as a mother Gronckle pushed her eggs into a pool. The eggs exploded underwater and out swam baby Gronckles.

"It's a good thing those don't hatch on Berk," Hiccup observed.

But little did Hiccup know that his friends had placed one of Meatlug's eggs in every hut in the village.

Astrid was pleased with her new tradition. Fishlegs agreed. "Everyone is going to be so surprised," he said giddily.

But instead of squeals of delight, explosions started going off throughout the village. That's when Astrid and Fishlegs figured out how baby Gronckles hatched.

"The eggs explode!" Astrid shouted. The villagers ran out of their huts to safety. This was not exactly the warm, fuzzy holiday tradition Astrid had hoped for.

Back on the island, the dragons and their babies were getting ready to go back home, to Berk. They wanted to be there in time for Snoggletog. The older dragons started to fly away, but the baby dragons were having trouble. They were still too little to fly.

Luckily Hiccup had an idea.

A few minutes later, everyone in Berk was staring up at the sky. Their dragons, and Hiccup, had returned. And they were hauling a ship filled with dragon babies!

"To the Great Hall!" announced Stoick. "We finally have something to celebrate!"

That evening, the Great Hall was filled with the sounds of happy Vikings and dragons. Everyone agreed that this was the best Snoggletog ever—everyone except Hiccup. Toothless was still nowhere to be found.

"Astrid, where did Toothless go?" Hiccup asked.

"I don't know," Astrid replied. But just as she finished speaking, the door to the Great Hall opened and in zoomed Toothless!

Hiccup gave his dragon a great big hug, and Toothless placed Hiccup's Snoggletog present right on his head. It was Hiccup's lost helmet!

Hiccup thanked Toothless. "You are amazing, bud."

"Happy Snoggletog!" shouted Astrid.

The next morning Toothless wanted to go for a ride, and he wanted to use his old tail, the one that Hiccup had to control.

"You don't need this anymore," Hiccup told him.

Toothless fanned out his new tail and then smashed it against the ground, staring at Hiccup all the while. Hiccup finally understood—his friend never wanted to fly without him ever again.

So Hiccup attached the old tail and off they went. It was indeed the best Snoggletog ever!